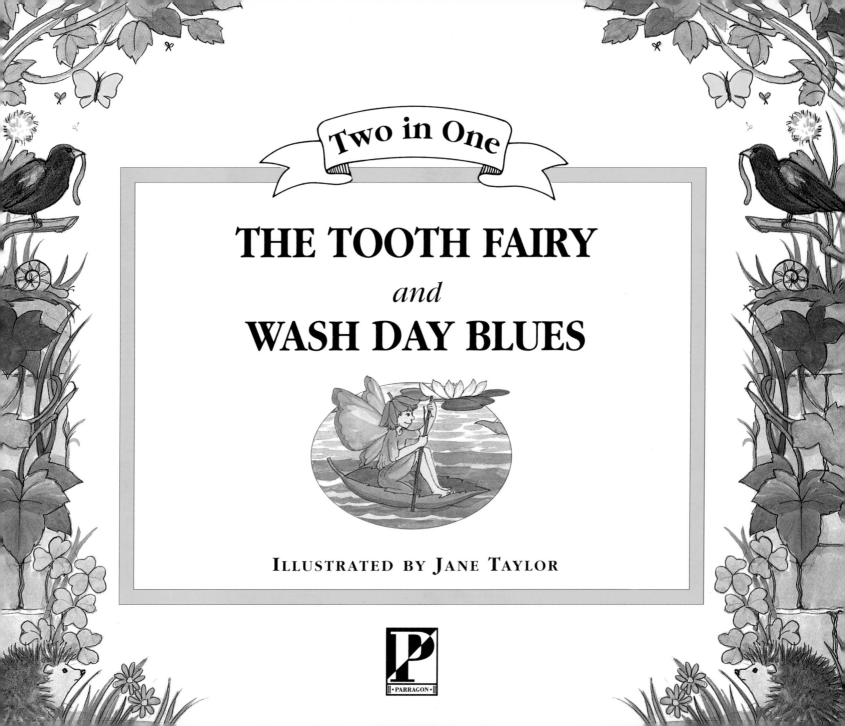

Two in One

THE TOOTH FAIRY

and

WASH DAY BLUES

ILLUSTRATED BY JANE TAYLOR

P
PARRAGON

This is a Parragon Book

©Parragon 1997

Parragon
13-17 Avonbridge Trading Estate
Atlantic Road, Avonmouth
Bristol. BS11 9QD

Produced by The Templar Company plc,
Pippbrook Mill, London Road, Dorking,
Surrey RH4 1JE

Designed by Janie Louise Hunt
Edited by Caroline Steeden
Printed and bound in Italy
ISBN 0 75252 501 8

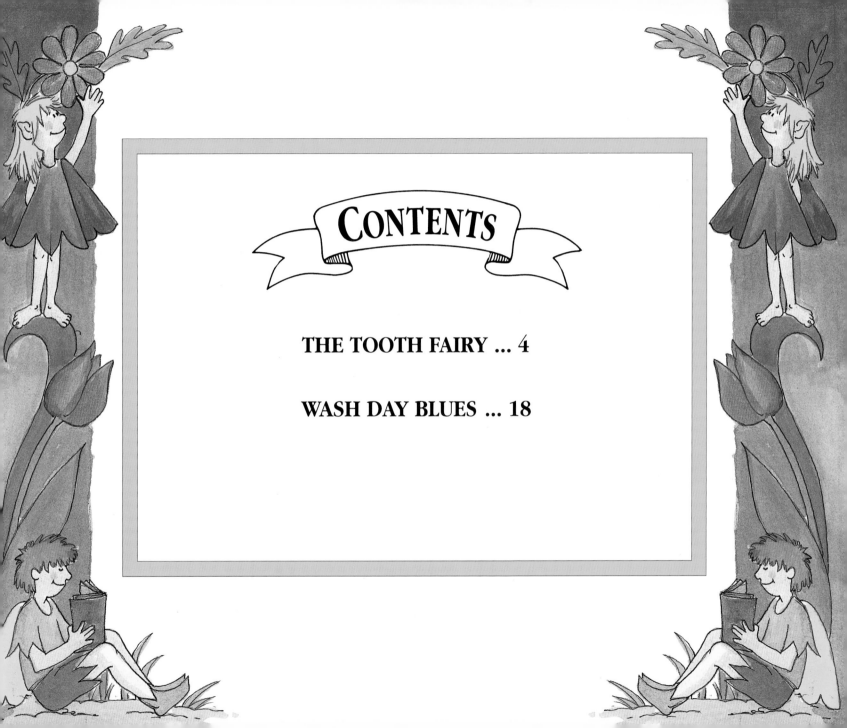

CONTENTS

THE TOOTH FAIRY

WRITTEN BY CANDY WALLACE

It all began when Thomas Timpson went to tea with his Grandma. Thomas's Grandma made very nice teas — well, almost! She made little squidgy sandwiches and wibbly-wobbly green jellies and strawberry milkshakes so frothy you got pink bubbles on the end of your nose. And she made rock cakes. Grandma's rock cakes were like — um— rocks. If you dropped one, Grandma's best china shook and rattled on the sideboard and her cat, Tibbles, ran in terror to hide under the sofa.

One day, when Thomas Timpson went to tea and bit into one of Grandma's rock cakes, his wobbly tooth came out and dropped onto his plate with a clink.

"Lucky Thomas!" said Grandma, "Let me put that tooth in a napkin for you. You must take it home and put it under your pillow for the Tooth Fairy!"

When Grandma disappeared into the kitchen, Thomas quickly popped the rest of his rock cake in the plant pot where Grandma's aspidistra grew. That's where he always put his rock cakes.

Thomas wasn't too sure about this Tooth Fairy business, but he was prepared to give it a try. So that night he put his tooth under his pillow and went to sleep.

The next morning, Thomas was amazed to find that his tooth had gone — and there was a shiny new coin lying in its place!

Thomas couldn't understand why anybody would want his old tooth, but he was very glad to have the coin. When he emptied his money-box he discovered there was nearly enough now to buy a new football!

The next week, to his delight, Thomas found that he had another wobbly tooth. He wiggled and jiggled it, but it just wouldn't budge.

"Mum," said Thomas, "please can I go to tea with Grandma?"

Grandma was pleased to see Thomas again. "I've made you some of your favourite rock cakes!" she said.

"What does the Tooth Fairy do with children's teeth, Grandma?" said Thomas, munching on a cheese and cucumber sandwich.

"You'll have to ask the Tooth Fairy," Grandma chuckled and went to get a fresh batch of rock cakes out of the oven.

"Now you tuck into those dear," said Grandma, "while I water my aspidistra, it's not looking at all well nowadays…"

Thomas closed his eyes tight and bit bravely into a cake. Hey, presto! Out came the tooth!

That night, Thomas didn't put the tooth under his pillow but instead decided to take Grandma's advice. He wrote a note which said:

"Dear Tooth Fairy, I do have a tooth for you but it's hidden. Wake me up and I'll tell you where it is. What do you want it for? Love Thomas."

And he settled down and went to sleep.

He was in the middle of a horrible dream where a giant rock cake with big teeth was trying to eat him when he suddenly woke up. He was amazed to see a tiny creature on his pillow, with miniature spectacles on her nose, reading his note and tutting to herself.

Thomas rubbed his eyes to make sure he wasn't still dreaming.

"Excuse me," he said, "are you the Tooth Fairy?"

"Yes I am, and after tonight I'm going to ask for a transfer to Dingly Dell duty. Dancing round a couple of toadstools is going to be a piece of cake after this job."

"I'll tell you where my tooth is if you tell me what you're going to use it for," said Thomas firmly.

"In my day children kept quiet and did as they were told," said the fairy, looking very cross. She put her spectacles away in a tiny pocket and folded her arms. "All right, it's a deal."

Thomas took his tooth from his bedside drawer and gave it to the fairy.

"But I don't have time to explain," she said. "You'll have to come and see for yourself."

Thomas was thrilled. "Will you whisk me off to Fairyland with a magic wand?" he asked excitedly, remembering the school play. Janice Potts had a wand to go with her fairy costume made out of a stick with a silver star on the end.

"You're a bit behind the times," sniffed the fairy, taking out a tiny remote control that sparkled in the moonlight. She pointed it at Thomas and pressed the button…

"WOW!" Thomas was standing in a vast room that sparkled and shone, as though covered with silvery cobwebs. In the middle of the room was a huge machine with a giant funnel at the top and a moving conveyor belt beneath. At the top of the funnel a big swinging bucket was filling up and emptying its cargo into the funnel. From the other end came a fine, sparkly powder that reflected all the colours of the rainbow. It flowed like a river along the conveyor belt to where it was dropped into little sacks and sealed.

Hundreds of fairies were busy everywhere, scurrying away with the sacks to load them onto little trollies, counting and making notes, bringing more supplies for the funnel. Dozens of little lights flashed on and off.

"See that funnel?" said the Tooth Fairy. "That's where your tooth will go. All the little teeth are dropped into there and what comes out the other end is magic powder. It's the secret ingredient in lots of our spells. We used pearls in the old days, but they're rather difficult to get hold of now."

mind the steps

"So now you use teeth!" exclaimed Thomas.

"Teeth are very valuable to us fairies," said the Tooth Fairy. "That's why we always pay you."

Thomas gazed in amazement at the sparkling scene. Magic powder hung in the air all around. When he looked down at his hand, it glittered in the silvery light.

"I have to take tonight's teeth to the stores," said the fairy, "and you must go back before morning. But since you're here, I'll grant you three wishes. We *had* cut wishes down to two but we've got a special offer on at the moment."

Thomas could hardly believe his ears. He closed his eyes and took a deep breath.

"I wish that I could buy my new football … and I wish that Grandma's rock cakes were light and fluffy … and I wish that her aspidistra would get better…"

Before he could finish speaking, the fairy factory had vanished. He was lying in his bed with the sun shining through his window. Feeling under the pillow, he felt a coin! Thomas rushed to his piggy bank and shook out all the money. He counted carefully. Yes! There was enough for the new football!

He took it round to Grandma's the following week when he went for tea. "Very nice, dear," said Grandma, as she brought in some delicious-smelling rock cakes fresh from the oven. Thomas sank his teeth into one and took a big bite. It was soft and crumbly, and full of big, juicy currants.

"These are great, Grandma!" he said in a mumbly sort of way because his mouth was full.

"Thank you, dear. It's a new recipe. Now you tuck in while I water my aspidistra — it's coming on a treat."

WASH DAY BLUES

WRITTEN BY CLAIRE STEEDEN

Wishy Washy the fairy lived and worked in fairyland. He owned a shop called Wishy's Washeteria which had a little flat above. He spent each day hand washing fairy wings, which was a very important job as you can imagine. Fairy wings are very expensive and Wishy took great pride in his job.

He was always very busy and today was no exception. At the weekend there was to be a huge party where the fairy council would announce which lucky fairies would

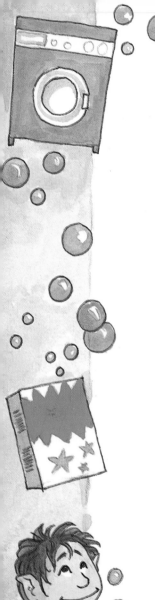

sit on top of the Christmas trees in people's homes at Christmas time. All day long fairies were coming in with sets of wings and asking if they would be ready by Saturday, as they wanted to look their best.

"Oh, I'll never wash all these wings in time," Wishy said to himself. "Each pair takes so long to do. It's Thursday afternoon already."

Wishy lifted a pair of wings gently into the tub, filled with warm water. He picked up a packet of Fairiel washing powder to sprinkle over the wings, but realized that it was empty.

"Oh, bother. That's all I need. Now what am I going to do. I've got a whole pile of wings to wash and no powder. I'll never have it all done by Saturday.

Wishy remembered seeing an advertisement in the newspaper for washing machines. "Maybe it's time I bought one," he thought. He found the paper and read the advertisement aloud.

"No more wash-day blues. Put a whizz into your wash with a brand new washing machine and let it work while you play!"

"Perfect. That's just what I need." Wishy phoned the company and they sent a fairy round to install one right away.

"Just read the instruction booklet and it will tell you how it works," said the plumber fairy, handing him a big box of powder.

"Thank you. I'll soon get all this washing done now," said Wishy.

After saying goodbye he went to look at his new machine. It was very big and covered in buttons and flashing lights. Wishy sat down and started to read the instructions, but they were far too complicated.

"It'll take me ages to work all of this out. If I just put it on a simple program it should be okay," Wishy said to himself. "Besides, I've got an important evening ahead and I must go and get ready. It's the final of the fairyland quiz competition tonight. If I win I can spend the money on a holiday. I haven't had one for years."

Wishy took all the wings off their hangers, loaded them into the machine, put in some of the new powder and set the machine on what he thought was a low setting. Then off he flew to the quiz, hoping to win the star prize so he could travel to the mountains.

Wishy took his seat just as the contest began. The host asked the contestants lots of questions, and to his surprise, Wishy ended up in the final three, with one tie-breaker question to answer:

"What," asked the fairy host, "is the highest mountain in Fairyland?"

"Mount Sparkle," answered Wishy.

"Correct. You've won the competition and a thousand fairy pieces!"

Everyone cheered, especially Wishy. He could have a holiday at last! He could not believe his luck. A lovely new washing machine and winning the competition all in one day! And to think he had been so miserable this morning.

Arriving home, he took off his wings and was just climbing into bed when he heard an awful rumbling noise coming from downstairs. Pulling on his dressing gown, Wishy went to investigate. The noise seemed to be coming from the laundry. Nervously, he stepped into the dark room.

"Yuk! What's that?" Wishy's feet were covered in something cold and tickly. He turned on the light and looked around. He couldn't believe his eyes. The whole floor was covered in soap suds, which were pouring out of his new machine. He ran to turn it off.

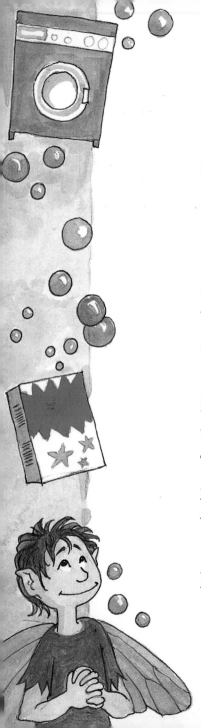

"Oh my goodness! What a mess. I hope the wings are all right," he said, opening the machine's door.

First of all he pulled out a pair that were enormous. "Oh, no. They've stretched. This pair are ruined. Oh dear!"

He reached in and pulled out another pair which looked the right size, but when he held them up they were full of holes. "Oh dear. They're all torn. I won't be able to mend holes that size," he sighed.

Suds were still oozing out onto the floor as he reached in and pulled out a bundle of wings. As he untangled them he let out a groan. "Ooh, all the colours have run. The new automatic powder I used can't have been right for these wings. The colours have mixed and made the wings patchy. What a disaster!" he cried.

Tears welled up in Wishy's eyes as he pulled out the last pair of wings. They were tiny.

"Oh dear. The water must have got too hot. It's shrunk this pair."

Wishy sat on his little wooden stool and cried, but his tears were lost amongst the bubbles. "All the wings are ruined and the fairies need them for Saturday. What am I going to do?" he wept.

Wishy spent all night clearing up the soapy mess.

"This will teach me not to be impatient. If I'd washed them by hand I wouldn't be in this mess," he said to himself. "I can't repair the wings, so I'll have to give each customer the money to buy a new pair. I'll have to use the money I won in the competition last night."

Wishy spent all the next day explaining to his customers about the machine and their ruined wings. After handing out money all day he only had twenty fairy pieces left of his prize money.

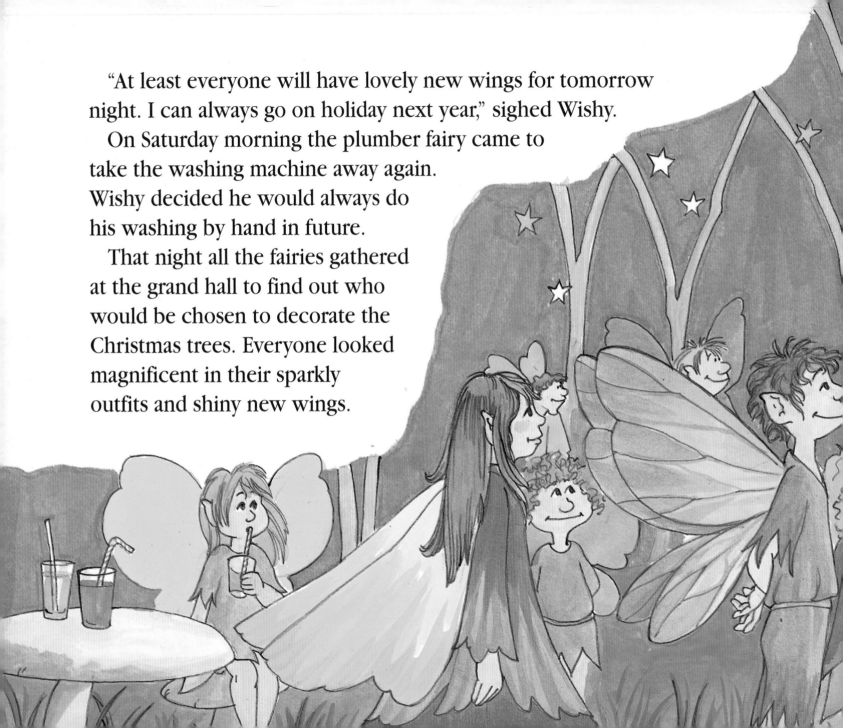

"At least everyone will have lovely new wings for tomorrow night. I can always go on holiday next year," sighed Wishy.

On Saturday morning the plumber fairy came to take the washing machine away again. Wishy decided he would always do his washing by hand in future.

That night all the fairies gathered at the grand hall to find out who would be chosen to decorate the Christmas trees. Everyone looked magnificent in their sparkly outfits and shiny new wings.

At eight o'clock a list of names was announced and there was much celebrating amongst the fairies. Just as Wishy was about to leave he heard his name being called out, and he turned to face the fairy speaker.

"Wishy, I understand that it is thanks to you that the fairies all have such beautiful new wings this evening," she said.

I hear you had an accident with your new washing machine, and you spent all the prize money you won in the quiz competition buying new wings for everybody. A thousand fairy pieces is a lot of money. I understand you wanted to spend it on a holiday in the mountains," said the fairy.

"Yes, that's right," replied Wishy.

"Well, you have proved what a hard working, kind and honest fairy you are. Your behaviour deserves some kind of reward." The fairy speaker handed Wishy an envelope.

"Here's some money that your friends and customers have collected for you. Everyone thinks you deserve a holiday, so you will make it to the mountains after all! Enjoy your trip."

Wishy thanked everybody, and when he got home he thought how lucky he was to have his little shop, such caring friends and a lovely holiday to look forward to.